P9-DDC-043

Dragonfly's Tale is based on an ancient Zuni story kept alive for centuries by tribal storytellers. It was first translated by anthropologist Frank Hamilton Cushing and published in *The Millstone* (Volume 9, 1884). In the hope of conveying this tale's important and timely message, I have simplified Cushing's version and added some details of my own. That is the way of storytellers. I think the Ancient Ones will understand.

K.R.

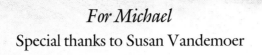

For Michael
Special thanks to Susan Vandemoer

Clarion Books
a Houghton Mifflin Company imprint
215 Park Avenue South, New York, NY 10003
Text and illustrations copyright © 1992 by Kristina Rodanas

All rights reserved.
For information about permission to reproduce
selections from this book, write to Permissions,
Houghton Mifflin Company,
215 Park Avenue South, New York, NY 10003.
Printed in the USA

Library of Congress Cataloging-in-Publication Data

Rodanas, Kristina.
Dragonfly's tale / retold and illustrated by Kristina Rodanas.
p.   cm.
Summary: After a poor harvest, two children regain the
Corn Maidens' blessings for their people with the aid of a cornstalk
toy, the dragonfly.
ISBN 0-395-57003-4   PA ISBN 0-395-72076-1
1. Zuni Indians—Legends.   [1. Zuni Indians—Legends.   2. Indians
of North America—New Mexico—Legends.]   I. Title.
E99.Z9R758 1992   90-28758
398.2—dc20   CIP   AC
[E]

HOR 10 9 8 7 6 5

DRAGONFLY'S TALE

Retold and Illustrated by

Kristina Rodanas

Clarion Books

NEW YORK

FRANKLIN PIERCE
COLL
RIN

Many lifetimes ago, in the days of the Ancient Ones, there lived a tribe of people known as the Ashiwi. Their village was called Hawikuh, and it sat at the top of a hill. The houses were built side by side, one upon another, in the shape of a great honeycomb.

Two powerful spirits, the Maidens of the White and Yellow Corn, watched over the village. Each spring, they sent warm winds to chase away the snow. In summer, they brought friendly rains to nourish the cornfields of Hawikuh.

The corn plants grew straight and strong with the Corn Maidens' blessings. Year after year, the people harvested more than they could eat, and the storerooms overflowed with corn.

One day, after the last of the ripe corn had been gathered and stored away, a group of children had a mud fight. Their laughter echoed down the narrow streets as they playfully threw lumps of dirt and mud.

The head chief of the tribe saw their game. Watching the children play, he thought of a plan to show off his people's wealth. He called a meeting of all the elders to share his scheme.

"The Ashiwi must celebrate their richest harvest with a mock battle," announced the chief. "Our weapons will be made of bread, batter, and dough. Let us invite our neighbors to take part. How they will envy our prosperity when they see us using our food for play!"

"Yes, yes," agreed the elders. "Let us begin!" And they praised the cleverness of their leader.

The elders ordered the people to prepare for the festivities.
The swiftest runners were sent to summon the guests from the
surrounding villages.

Excited, the people set to work chopping wood to fuel the ovens,
and grinding corn into meal. The cooking fires roared and crackled.
The air was sweet with the smell of baking bread and boiling mush.

On the day of the celebration, the Corn Maidens decided to go
to Hawikuh to see what the commotion was about. Disguised as
old and bedraggled women, they limped into town. No one noticed
the warm, misty wind that accompanied them.

9

At the crowded village plaza, the Corn Maidens paused to look around. Everywhere they saw bowls and baskets filled with batter and dough. Mounds of cakes steamed in the windows. Stacks of bread covered the housetops.

A boy and his little sister sat nearby munching corn cakes drenched in honey. When they saw how ragged and hungry the two women looked, they held out their hands to offer them some food. But one of the elders quickly snatched it away.

"Good food should not be wasted on beggars," he scolded. "These women are too lazy to grow their own corn. They are like hungry coyotes looking for an easy meal!"

Suddenly the plaza grew silent as the chief began to divide the people into teams. Then, with a nod of his head, the great battle began.

Everyone laughed as they ducked flying bread and biscuits. One team hurled balls of dough, while the other threw globs of batter. The invited neighbors stared in bewilderment as their hosts smeared each other with precious food.

The Corn Maidens watched the fight with heavy hearts. They had blessed the Ashiwi with an abundance of food. But the people had thrown away their gifts.

"It is time to teach our children a lesson," said one Maiden to the other. Then, like windblown smoke, they vanished.

When the games ended, the guests went home in disgust. While the moon rose over the town, the seed-eaters scampered into the plaza. Silently, armies of mice, gophers, bugs, and birds carried away every crumb of food. Then they tunneled into the storerooms and stole the corn. They worked all through the night, for the Corn Maidens had warned them that a great famine was soon to come to the village of Hawikuh.

The people could hardly believe their eyes the next morning. All the wasted food that had covered the village streets had disappeared. The storerooms were half empty.

"Who cares?" they asked one another. "We have more than enough corn to last through the winter, until our next great harvest!"

Winter came, and was slow to pass. Warm winds arrived late, and the rains never fell to moisten the soil.

The priests sang their most sacred chants and danced their most powerful rituals. But the Corn Maidens refused to send their blessings. The corn plants grew weak and withered in the hot, cracked earth.

Their storerooms bare, the people ate cactus and ground bones. Autumn arrived, then winter, and the famine deepened. The snows came and were heavier than anyone could recall.

What was to be done? The chief called together a council.

"We will go to our neighbors for help," he declared. "If we delay, we will starve. We must leave for their village tonight!"

The people rushed to collect their warmest robes and blankets. They hurried from their homes and scrambled into the icy darkness.

In one house, a boy and his little sister were forgotten. No one had noticed them sleeping beside the hearth.

When the boy woke up, he climbed the ladder to the sky hole and gazed all around. The village was empty!

Although he was frightened, he knew he would need to comfort his sister. Perhaps he could make a beautiful toy, something to remind her of happier times.

"I know," he whispered. "I will make her a butterfly!"

While the little girl slept, the boy set to work. He carved the butterfly's body from the core of a dry cornstalk, and made its legs from straw. Carefully, he cut the wings out of a brittle corn leaf. The leaf was narrow, so he had to make long, slender wings.

Then he painted the insect with bright colors. The thin pigment spread out, making the eyes very large, and forming a delicate pattern of lines in the corn-leaf wings.

The boy admired his creation. Although it did not look exactly like a butterfly, it was certainly a wonderful creature.

When she heard that they were alone in the village, the little girl began to cry. But the cornstalk creature helped her forget her sadness. All day she played with the beautiful toy, which twirled round and round at the end of a long thread. That night, just before sleep, the child said to the creature, "Please fly away and find us some food to eat!"

For a moment, it seemed the brittle wings fluttered, as if the toy had heard her request.

Later, while his sister slept, the boy heard a soft buzzing sound. "*Thli ni ni*," it said. "Let me go!"

Looking up, he saw his butterfly spinning in the moonlight. Its wings were beating wildly. He reached out to calm the strange creature, then carefully untied it.

"*Thli ni ni ni*," hummed the insect, darting around the room. With a twang like a bowstring, it shot straight up through the sky hole and soared into the night.

The creature flew south to the Land of Everlasting Summer, where the Corn Maidens lived. When he neared their home, he was tired from his long journey. For an instant he rested upon the silken tassel of a corn plant. Then he flew to another, and another, and in this way he finally came to the Corn Maidens' dwelling.

The creature found the two spirits strolling through the green fields. He told them all about the boy and his sister.

"We will gladly help the two little ones," said the Maiden of the Yellow Corn. "There was once a time when they offered us food. We have not forgotten their kindness." Then the Maidens summoned their messengers and directed them to deliver food to the children.

The creature thanked the Corn Maidens and happily hummed his way back to Hawikuh.

When the children woke up, the house was filled with baskets of beans and squash. A mound of corn reached to the ceiling. The boy and his sister danced for joy.

But where was the cornstalk creature? The little girl found him in a dark corner, perched on a painted jar. He sat very still, as though he knew nothing at all about the mysterious food delivery.

Brother and sister had plenty to eat in the days that followed. As time passed, winter waned. A warm wind blew in from the south and melted away the snow.

One morning, the children went out to plant corn. The boy sprinkled a handful of cornmeal onto the ground and thanked the Corn Maidens for their blessings. Then he poked deep holes in the dirt and dropped in the seed corn. The little girl covered the kernels with earth.

That night, a misty rain fell over Hawikuh. By morning, the children were surprised to see that tiny corn plants had shot through the soil. Long, wavy leaves appeared the next day, and on the third morning silver tassels bloomed. When the sun rose on the fourth day, the plants had sprouted heavy ears of white and yellow corn.

Happily, brother and sister picked the ripest ears, dug a pit, and roasted them. Filled with fresh corn, they fell asleep.

As the children slept, the Ashiwi returned to Hawikuh. Humbled by the great famine, they had come to replant their fields, hoping for an ample harvest.

When they saw the ripening corn, the people were astonished. "We have been blessed by the Corn Maidens," they said to one another.

One of the elders had noticed the brother and sister sleeping at the edge of the cornfield. The little girl was holding a wonderful toy—an insect made of cornstalk. "These two children are the ones who have been blessed," he declared.

The chief stepped forward. "Let us honor the Corn Maidens, and let us learn from the children who have received their gifts," he said. "Then, perhaps we, too, may share in the blessing."

From then on, the people were careful not to take the Corn Maidens' gifts for granted. They respected the boy and his sister, and learned their ways of kindness. The cornfields thrived, and all the Ashiwi prospered.

And what became of the cornstalk creature? To this day, in early summer—when the corn is beginning to bloom—he appears. Never content with his resting place, he hums from one corn tassel to the next.

He is known as Dragonfly.